THE BOOK OF CLOUDS

First published in Great Britain in 2018 by the Emma Press
Originally published in 2010 as *Mākoņu grāmata* by Liels un mazs

Text © Juris Kronbergs
Illustrations © Anete Melece
English language translation © Māra Rozīte & Richard O'Brien

A CIP catalogue record of this book is available
from the British Library

Supported by Latvian Writers' Union (*Latvijas Rakstnieku savienība*)
and Ministry of Culture of the Republic of Latvia

Printed in Latvia by *Jelgavas tipogrāfija*

All rights reserved.

ISBN 978-1-910139-14-1

THE EMMA PRESS LTD
Registered in England and Wales, no. 08587072
Website: theemmapress.com
Email: queries@theemmapress.com
Jewellery Quarter, Birmingham, UK

The Book of Clouds

Poems by
Juris Kronbergs

Illustrated by
Anete Melece

Translated by
Māra Rozīte and Richard O'Brien

CONTENTS

Clouds in the sky	2
What do you think?	7
It's easy for clouds	8
Encyclopedias	12
There are, of course, many more	15
Cloud grammar	18
Cloud flags	19
Clouds follow	21
Travellers	22
Hail	24
Your own little cloud	25
Clouds are gourmands	26
The tropical island	28
Which was the very first cloud?	29

The dream	30
Rain like piano chords	32
Cloud vitamins	34
The trip	35
Cloud dances	36
Autumn	38
This	39
Clouds are	40
Now it's night	41
A cloud never dies	44
When all the clouds	46
My clouds: *write, draw or stick things in!*	49

About the poet	58
About the illustrator	59
About the translators	60

BONUS BITS

Learn some Latvian	64
Write your own poem!	65
About the Emma Press	70
Other books from the Emma Press	71

'Hey, cloud above me, big and full –
what makes you so beautiful?'

'You – you do!
I see you there:
small as a spot, round as a dot!'

Clouds in the sky

Clouds in the sky go to and fro
and watch us from above;
they hear us laugh or row
from up above.

Do they or don't they know
what's really going on below?
Year after year,
they go to and fro.

Some clouds are rich, some only pour.
They never stay the way
they looked before: their norm
is to keep changing form.
You get the drift – they shape-shift.

Clouds can be big as a barn
or smaller than a gnat.
Largely, they're quite relaxed

but some still glumly stare
or grumble up aloft,
drippily talking hot air
until everyone's dropped off.

Clouds are odd-bods. Some come over all
blundering and thundering,
while others hardly crawl.

So when you feel a shadow
passing overhead,
it might just be a cloud that wants
to say 'Hello!' instead.

What do you think?

A cloud, of course, is easy to find,
but do you know what goes on in its mind?

If it's sad, tears tumble.
If it's glad, it might chuckle.
If it's mad, it'll grumble and rumble.

But what do you think it actually thinks
of the part it's asked to play – that sphinx
with an impish glint in its sliver
of silver lining?

Can that ever be seen, what it's thinking?
Well – you might get an inkling,
with the slightest sprinkling
when a cloud comes clean.

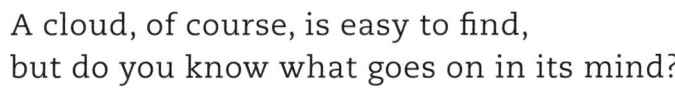

It's easy for clouds

It's easy for clouds to play pretend!
But they don't ever
do it to offend.

It's just such heavenly fun, or so I'm told:
Never gets old!

I don't know how,
but clouds can change
from their own selves to something strange:
a snake, a cake, a crow,
a crown, a car, a calf,
half a giraffe, a cart,
a carton or a tart.

I once knew a cloud
that turned into a song,
with a maudlin cloudy chorus.

It was so moved
as it crooned its tune
tears welled up
till the cloud cried itself out

Encyclopedias

In encyclopedias you can read,
if you desire, the names of clouds:
they're very strange indeed.

Veil clouds
Cirrostratus

High-heap clouds
Altocumulus

Thunderclouds
Cumulonimbus

Shelved-heap clouds

Heap clouds
Cumulus

Now listen, and I'll tell you what
each cloud is for, from dark to white,
and what they want:

With *Feather clouds*
long ago clouds wrote poems and prose

Lamb's wool clouds
line nightgowns and cloud-covers

Veil clouds are needed at weddings by brides
or if there's something they have to hide

High-heap clouds are
stacks of cloudstraw

Shelf clouds are all found high up
on cloudcastle walls

Rainclouds are what clouds wear in showers:
their coats, the way cagoules are ours.

Heap clouds rarely sleep,
but bounce and bob and leapfrog,
navel-gazing at the cloudfluff
in their bellybuttons.

Thunderclouds police the skies

And *Snowclouds* shovel snowdrifts
from the streets and squares of cloudtowns.

There are, of course, many more

There are, of course, many more clouds
these reference books don't speak about:

there's *Western clouds*
and *Cluster-clouds*
and, if I remember rightly,
Flustered clouds and *Bluster-clouds*.

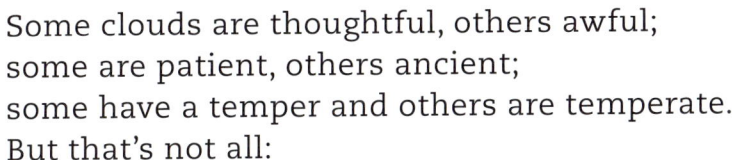

Some clouds are thoughtful, others awful;
some are patient, others ancient;
some have a temper and others are temperate.
But that's not all:

There's *Car-clouds* that drive cloudy Audis;
City-clouds in high-rise blocks;
Farming-clouds that harvest crops;
Splinter-clouds that stab your socks;
and then there's *Coarse clouds, Of course clouds, Off-course clouds,
His-and-hers clouds, Now and then clouds,
Yes* and *No* and *Maybe clouds* and clouds for *Come again?*
Oh yes, it's true, we do have clouds
of every species, strain and hue:

like *Hurry-scurry clouds,
Cloud-tanks* and *Cloud-banks*
that know all there is to know
about cloud money.

(Cloud money, by the way,
looks and behaves
a lot like hail.)

contrail

↑
HALF-CLOUD

FRAGMENT OF SNOT-CLOUD

draine

though
cloud

Shy evening cloud

h January -005 - g covered city

CLOUD OF DOUBT

PYROCUMULUS

STINK POTS

The famous weather-forecast cloud

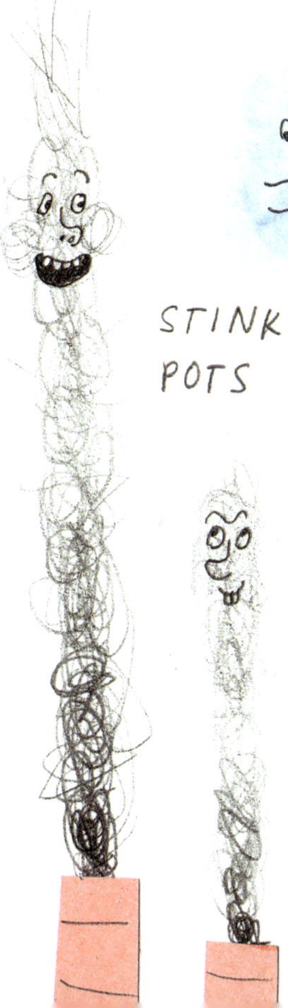

↑
ZIG-ZAG CLOUD

Cloud grammar

Of course it's only a suggestion
but I'd rather you didn't question
the need to study the grammar of the clouds.

First, there are *Whereclouds,*
Thereclouds, Whenclouds and
Thenclouds
(as well as *Whither* and *Thitherclouds*).
Then we have *Howclouds* and also *Nounclouds*
that like to find people, places and things
and give them all names: like Vikings and strings,
like bananas and the Bahamas.

Placename clouds
like to stay in one spot,
rain down heavily
and not move a jot.

There are also philosophical
Truefalseclouds,
Mediator clouds, Debater clouds,
subtle, supple *Rebuttal clouds,*
Can and *Kant clouds*
and *Ant clouds.*

Ant clouds?

Yes – don't tell me that you've never seen
the crowd of clouds that scramble up an anthill?

Cloud flags

When clouds have their flags fluttering,
it means the clouds are gathering
right in your neighbourhood.

They've all been summoned to discuss
things that have nothing to do with us:

the dangers posed
by sun dogs and high mountain snows,
and how to get the winds to slow;
the vexing questions
of air-space congestion

that dog their days –
that's to say
what they are and what they will become.

These meetings don't get acrimonious,
since clouds are mostly very courteous –
but they're long-winded, and they're tedious.

Rain and sleet
start falling when they fall asleep.

If *Walkingclouds* start walking off,
and if the *Rainclouds* sob,
cats cry; we fly
when it rains cats and dogs.

Clouds follow

Clouds follow a falling barometer
like people follow
falling stocks and shares.

And some clouds watch barometer conditions
the way some people watch out
for police and politicians.

Travellers

Most clouds travel back and forth
across the earth:
migrating, relocating,
crisscrossing the sky
in a vast cloud flyby.

And some clouds clown around:
they back-flip, flip-flop, side-slip,
drift up, up and over an updraft,
then raft down the air troughs:
what show-offs!

Great globe-trotters,
clouds knew the world was round
before word got around on the ground.
They were the first
citizens of the world:
champions of organisations
like the European Cloud Union*
and the United Cloud Formations.**

The European Cloud Union has its headquarters in Frankfurt, in the clouds above where the European Central Bank is located.

**Situated in New York about a mile above the UN skyscraper, by the East River.*

Hail

Sometimes quiet, rarely loud,
white hail drops down from the clouds.

Sometimes hailstones are small
as fleas, and other times they fall
as big and round as bowling balls.

How long do they roll around
on the ground?
Not long: in moments
their components
have dissolved into steam
and streamed up in the air
and become a new cloud
somewhere up there.

Your own little cloud

Sometimes, the sky looks clear
without a cloud at all,
but still grey rains fall.

And wherever you go,
a little cloud follows like a shadow.

Is it imagined, or real?
Perhaps it's all your cares and troubles,
snapping at your heels…

Could you pack this cloud in an old kit-bag
like all your troubles in the song they sang?
Or will this trouble-cloud keep bubbling on?

Clouds are gourmands

They eat pie-in-the-sky
with float potatoes
and scarlet sunset cream.

Some clouds prefer
Black Forest gateaux
from alpine plateaus.

And then, disguised as fog,
they sneak around allotment plots

to pluck blackberries and blueberries,
raspberries and cloudberries,
and on the spot, they simply scoff the lot.

The tropical island

Once I was on a tropical isle
where the sky and sea stretched out for miles,

where the fields were ploughed
and the clouds as thin as shrouds.

There was never a change in the weather:
never rain, or fog, or thunder,
and all the songs there sang about
this wonder.

There were no winter days as dark as caves.
It never snowed.
No one froze or was ever chilled to the bone.

Thin veils of cloud just fluttered and faded,
fluttered and faded to a breeze
sowing the seeds of its heat on these southerly seas.

Which was the very first cloud?

Which cloud was
the very first one?

What did it think?

It might have felt friendless and alone
in the endless, empty sky,
and decided to cry

over the earth,
drop in on the dinosaurs
so small it hadn't noticed them before –
and the even smaller things
that lived next door.

The dream

Once a cloud
had a nightmare.

It dreamt
of the sun growing hotter and hotter,
and felt
itself getting smaller and smaller.

It risked disappearing completely.

It looked around, and found
that it was all alone.

All other clouds
were being stuffed into the sun's
huge yellow mouth.

Then all at once it heard a voice nearby:
'Wakey wakey, rise and shine!'

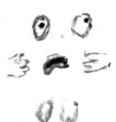

Rain like piano chords

And rain fell like piano chords:
arpeggios in shifting tempos on pools and lagoons,
on blades of grass, the leaves of trees,
on pine needles, on sand and mud,
often accompanied by thunderdrum.
Is that how cloudmusic first began?

Is that how music itself began?
A cloud-conductor leading a Cloud Symphony
scored and arranged by Cloudwig van Rainhoven.

These strains were heard by plants and birds,
and maybe this is why without rain
nothing flows or grows:
in deserts, for example,
where clouds rarely dare to tread,
because you have to travel by camel there
and, as you know, camels give clouds the hump.

Cloud vitamins

Healthy cloud drops are, for example, A and B, and C, and D.

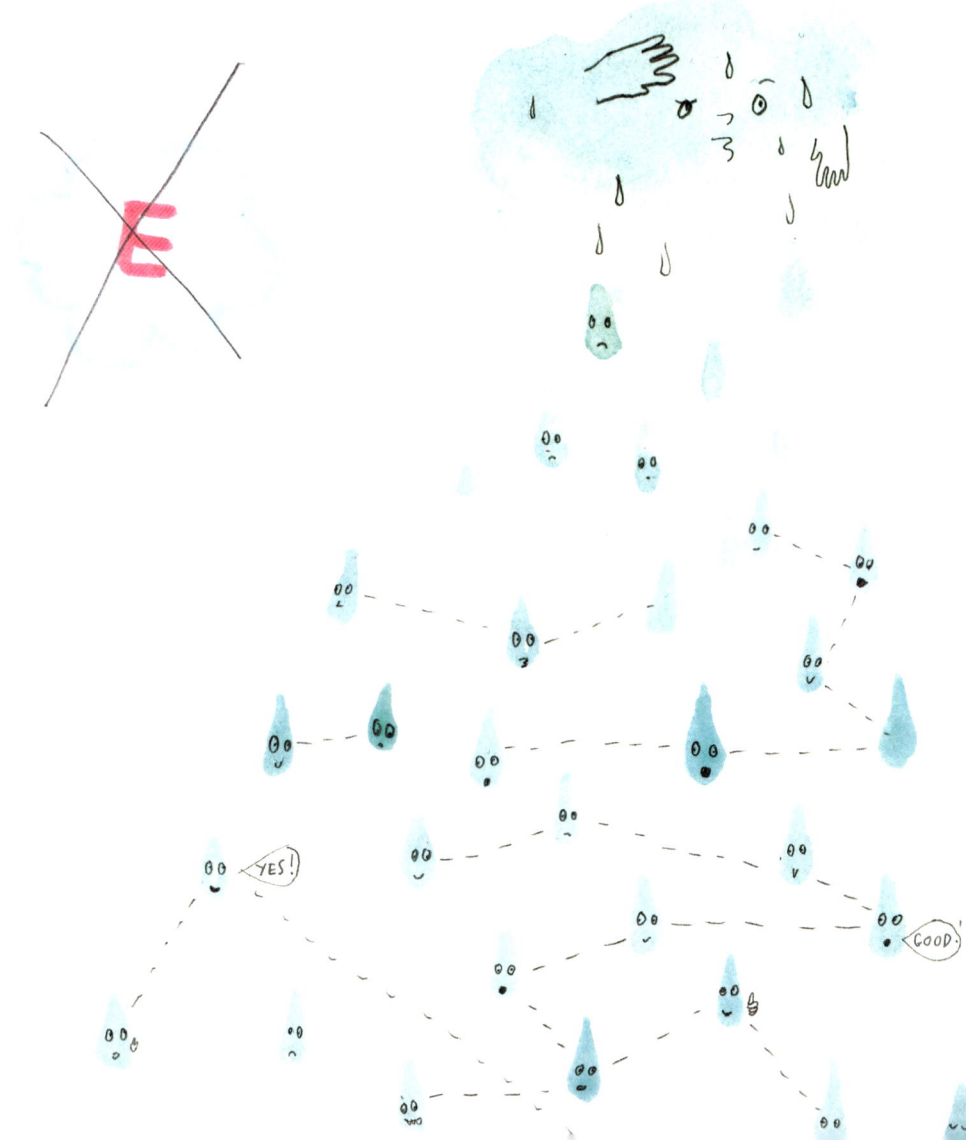

The trip

A cloud once wanted
to travel the world.
It hopped into a bi-plane
and took the southern skyway.

But on the way it got so hot
it broke up into droplets
which dripped onto the ground.

There all the droplets connected
to the cloud and called each other up
on their drop-phones

to get back together
after they'd evaporated.
So that's exactly what they did.

Soon they were joined by other drops
from other clouds,
and all the drops agreed
that no one could remember

which cloud each belonged to first,
and in the end, it didn't really matter.

Cloud dances

Some nights
clouds hold
dances and discos,
put on bright
red threads
and line-dance
along the horizon.
This can be seen
from Rīga to Bled.
That's why
some sunsets
glow so red.

Autumn

Now autumn's here again:
the air grows cool,
the days are shortening
and the clouds –
the clouds start looking
more and more like snow.

Winter's on its way,
and rays of sun go flashing by
like snowboarders,
they pass so fast.

Moreover, you yourself decide
what to see outside –

so even sunrays could come to a stop
and for a while
enjoy the peace of autumn.

The evening floats down slowly
like a huge dark leaf.

You might feel a little drop,
look up
and see a host of fluffy, friendly clouds.

Warm greetings from a great height,
out of the cold
as the year grows old.

This

What can clouds teach us?
Not much. Just this:

that fast or slow,
changes hardly show.
Sooner or later
everything must go.

MAP OF THE CLOUDINESS OF THE WORLD

(in October when the clouds
are in bloom)

Clouds are

Clouds are
between us and the sun,
although
having seen them
for a thousand years,
it's still not clear
if they are there
to shelter us
from getting scorched
by too much sun

or if

behind the clouds, the sun
is sheltering from us.

Or else – we're here
to give the clouds something
to brighten up their days.

Now it's night

Now that it's night,
the clouds are in their deep, dark beds,

except those few
who stay awake
to watch over the moon.

That's right:
it's night.
And now a single cloud's
reading the moon a bedtime story
about the earth and sky.

The fable's words
are able to give life
to life on earth.

A cloud never dies

A cloud
can never die;
winds scatter it
across the sky

and later it
returns
in a new place
in a new form.

13:5

14:0

14:21

14:28

14:44

14:50

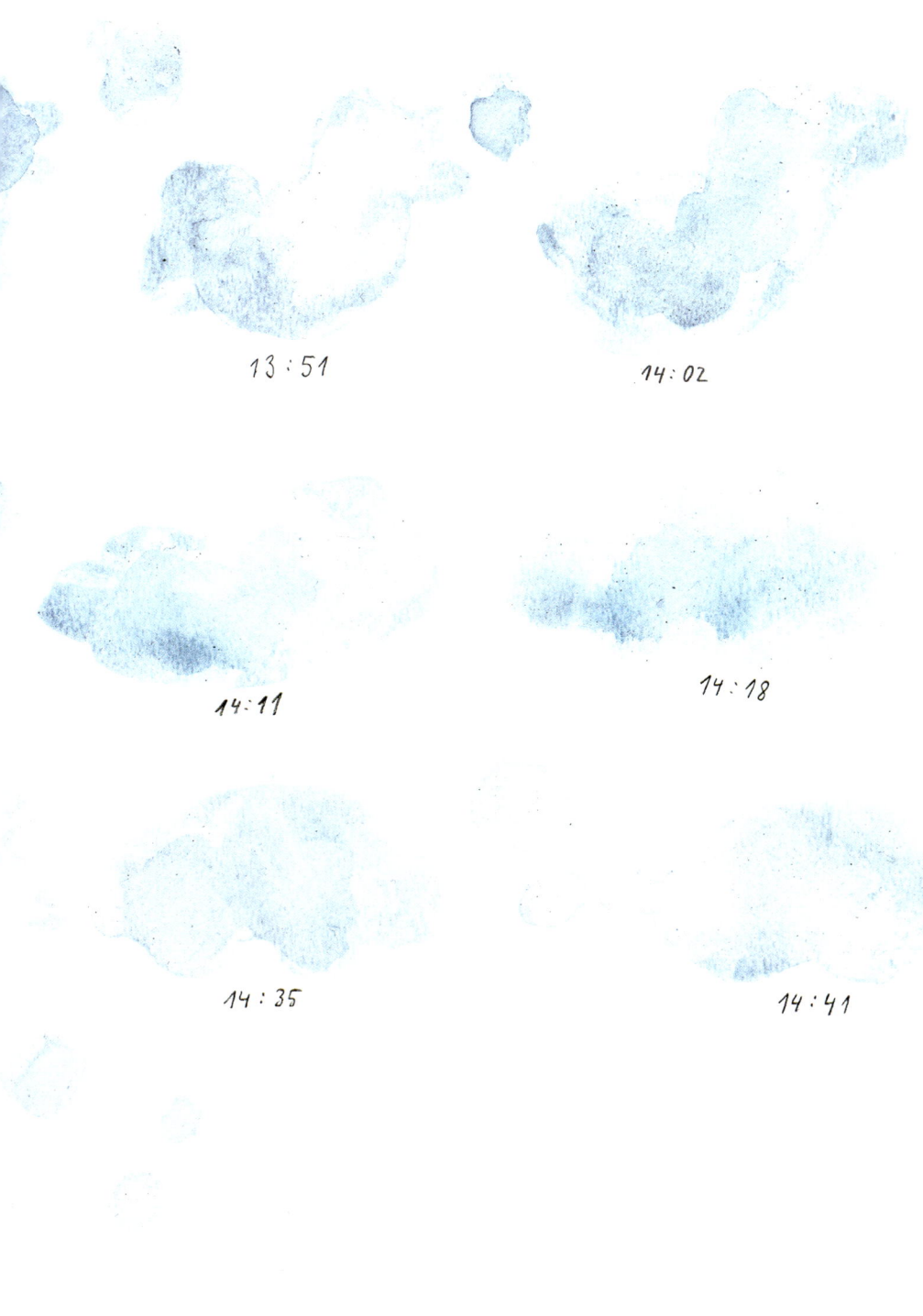

When all the clouds

When all the clouds unlock
their windows and unblock

      their doors – that's when
      the sky is blue again.

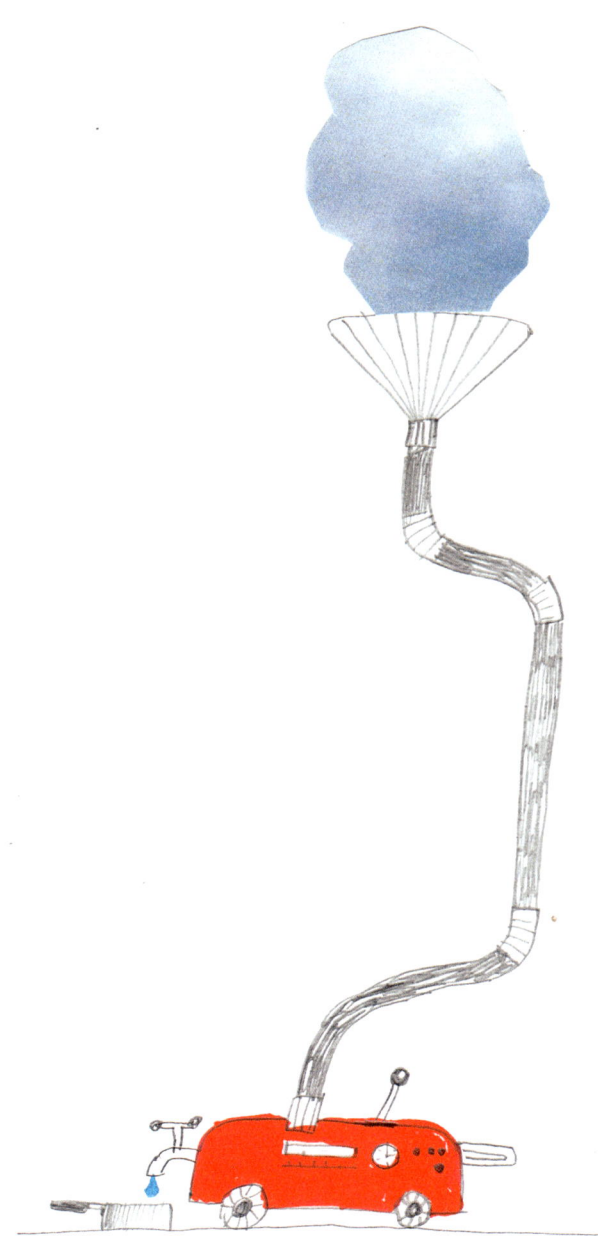

MY CLOUDS

Write, draw or stick things in!

Where, when, what time did you see it?
What type of cloud?
What does it do?
What does it eat?
Any other characteristics.

Write, draw or stick things in!

Write, draw or stick things in!

Write, draw or stick things in!

Write, draw or stick things in!

Write, draw or stick things in!

Write, draw or stick things in!

Write, draw or stick things in!

Write, draw or stick things in!

ABOUT THE POET

Juris Kronbergs is a poet and translator. He was born in Sweden in 1946, to a family of Latvian artists.

He studied Literature, Science, Nordic and Baltic languages at the University of Stockholm, and the Theory of Translation and 20th-century Poetry at the University of Cambridge, UK.

He has worked as a radio journalist, interpreter, diplomat and lecturer, and he has published sixteen poetry collections and sixty books of translations.

His poems have been translated into many languages: English, Swedish, German, French, Italian, Norwegian, Danish, Icelandic, Finnish, Estonian, Lithuanian, Czech, Polish, Russian, Ukrainian, Armenian, Greek, Slovenian, Catalan, Irish, Welsh, Chinese and Korean.

Juris has been awarded the Latvian Three Star Order, the Swedish North Star Order, and several scholarships and prizes, including the prize for best poetry collection of the year in Latvia for his collections *Wolf One-Eye* (1997) and *On the Balcony* (2017).

Photo: from the author's personal archive

ABOUT THE ILLUSTRATOR

Anete Melece was born in 1983. She is a Latvian illustrator and animation filmmaker based in Zürich, Switzerland. She studied visual communication at the Art Academy of Latvia and animation at Lucerne University of Applied Sciences and Art.

So far, Anete has illustrated five children's books and created three animated shorts. Her animated shorts have been screened at film festivals all around the world and have received numerous awards, including the Swiss Film Award for Best Animation in 2014 for 'The Kiosk' and the Animated Grand Prix at Encounters 22nd Short Film and Animation Festival 2016 for 'Analysis Paralysis'.

You can see more of her work on her website: http://www.anetemelece.lv/

Photo: Atis Jākobsons

ABOUT THE TRANSLATORS

Māra Rozīte was born in 1952 in Sydney, Australia, to parents who were refugees from Soviet Latvia after WWII.

She studied drama at Flinders University (South Australia) and moved to Sweden in 1980 to study Baltic languages at Stockholm University.

She has worked as an actor, theatre director, set and costume designer, radio journalist for Radio Sweden and has written a number of playscripts in Latvian. She has translated a number of Latvian poets into English including Juris Kronbergs' *Wolf One-Eye*, which was published by Arc Publications in 2006 as part of their Visible Poets series.

She is currently teaching in a primary school in Stockholm.

Photo: Egils Kronbergs

Richard O'Brien is a poet, playwright, translator and academic.

His pamphlets include *The Emmores* (Emma Press, 2014) and *A Bloody Mess* (Valley Press, 2015). His work has featured in *Oxford Poetry, Poetry London* and *The Salt Book of Younger Poets*. In 2017, he won an Eric Gregory Award.

He also writes for children: his first children's play – an adaptation of *The Selfish Giant* – was produced at the Arcola Theatre in 2016.

He is a Teaching Fellow in Creative Writing at the University of Birmingham.

Photo: John Canfield

BONUS BITS

LEARN SOME LATVIAN

Now that you've read some Latvian poems, how about learning the language? We've picked out some words that were in the original Latvian text, along with how to say them (in brackets). Put the emphasis on the CAPITALS and try to roll your *rrrrr*s a bit.

- **mākonis** (MAK-oh-niece) .... cloud
- **debess** (DEH-bess) .... sky
- **laiks** (LIKES) .... weather
- **lietus** (LEE-et-oos) .... rain
- **saule** (SA-oo-luh) .... sun
- **sniegs** (znEEgs) .... snow
- **pērkons** (PEAR-cons) .... thunder
- **krusa** (CROO-sah) .... hail
- **zeme** (ZEH-muh) .... earth/the ground
- **lidmašīna** (leed-mah-SHE-nah) .... aeroplane

WRITE YOUR OWN POEM!

Fancy writing your own poem and then maybe illustrating it too? Translator Richard O'Brien has come up with some ideas to help get you started.

Lots of the poems in this book wonder what clouds might think of us – for example, in '**Clouds in the sky**' (page 2). Of course, we'll probably never know what clouds think, but there are lots of other things in the world that might have their own ideas too.

Write a poem from the perspective of something else – a river, a mountain, a skyscraper, anything – exploring what it might think about us humans.

The poem '**Encyclopedias**' (page 12) gives us a list of real types of cloud, and then in the next poem (page 15) Juris makes up some types of cloud and talks about their characteristics. Let's make up some clouds of our own...

Next time you're outside, **look up at a cloud and try to describe what it looks like** – some examples from the book are 'car clouds' and 'ant clouds'.

Then think about how it might behave. If your cloud is a whale, how would it feel slowly drifting around the sky? Would it be like a whale in the sea, or very different? If your cloud is a turkey, does it cluck and gobble? How do the other clouds feel about this?

Look at '**Travellers**' on page 22. This poem talks about the places clouds go in their life, and how easily they move around the world. You might not have gone as far as they can, but you can still imagine what it might be like.

Pick a place you know – somewhere near you, like a park or a swimming pool, or maybe somewhere you've been on holiday or to visit family.

Describe what that place might look like from up above, to a cloud – especially a busy cloud with other places to be! What does it think of everything (and everyone) it sees?

Try not to think about the place the way *you* see it, but get inside the head of the cloud.

We can all picture clouds changing when we watch them in the sky – but sometimes words change too. This book is a translation from Latvian into English, which means me and my fellow translator Mara had to find words in English that had the same effect as the words in Latvian.

It can be tricky to do this, because a lot of poetry is about sound – what words sound nice together, whether they share an opening letter (alliteration) or the whole words sound similar out loud (rhyme).

One poem in the book, '**It's easy for clouds**' (page 8), features a list of words that sound good together, but are otherwise unconnected! Take a look:

> a snake, a cake, a crow,
> a crown, a car, a calf,
> half a giraffe, a cart,
> a carton or a tart.

Put together your own list of things changing into other things, where you let the letters and the rhythm help you choose the words. If you need something to kick you off, try this:

> Clouds can change
> from their own selves to something strange:
>
> a box, a fox, a frog,
> a log, a [......], a [......]

At the end of '**It's easy for clouds**' (page 8), the cloud 'cries itself out' and the illustrator Anete makes this something you can see on the page by having the writing G R A D U A L L Y   D I S A P P

This makes it feel like just at that moment, the poem is the cloud. It's a piece of writing and a piece of art at the same time.

Write a poem about a cloud and try to make how it *looks* on the page reflect what's going on in the words.

Juris uses clouds as a way to talk about other things in '**Clouds follow**' (page 21). The clouds in this poem pay attention to changes in the weather, and Juris points out that some people pay attention to political changes in the same way.

This might be especially important in a country like Latvia, which unlike Britain has been ruled by lots of different types of government.

Could you **make a similar comparison, between something seemingly unimportant and something quite serious** – like football and war, or ice cream and global warming? When you've got your two ideas, write a short poem that shows how they relate to each other.

In '**This**' (page 39), Juris asks what clouds can teach us and offers one possible answer: they can help us learn a lesson about change.

I like this idea of things outside in the world being able to teach us different things to what we're taught in school. It's not just clouds – frogs can teach us, and flowers, and bugs too.

Think closely about something you see in the world and think about what it might be able to teach us. You could start with a version of the original question, e.g. 'What can bugs teach us?' Then give your own short response.

In the poem about clouds, the answer seems especially neat because it rhymes all the way through – the words 'slow', 'show' and 'go' sound similar, so they tie the whole idea together. See if you can try the same thing: make your lesson even more memorable by picking words that rhyme.

We'd love to see what you come up with in response to these prompts! If you'd like us to take a look, email your poems and pictures to hello@theemmapress.com with 'The Book of Clouds' in the subject line.

ABOUT THE EMMA PRESS

The Emma Press is a publishing house based in Birmingham, UK. It makes books for adults and children, and specialises in poetry.

Emma Press books are starting to win prizes, including the Poetry Book Society Pamphlet Choice Award and the Saboteur Award for Best Collaborative Work. Having been shortlisted for the Michael Marks Award for Poetry Pamphlet Publishers in both 2014 and 2015, the Emma Press finally won it in 2016 (hurray!).

Falling Out of the Sky: Poems about Myths and Monsters, the first Emma Press poetry book for children, was shortlisted for the 2016 CLiPPA, run by the Centre for Literacy in Primary Education. *Moon Juice*, a collection of poems by Kate Wakeling with illustrations by Elīna Brasliņa, won the CLiPPA in 2017.

You can find out more about the Emma Press and buy books directly from us here:

theemmapress.com

ALSO FROM THE EMMA PRESS

THE NOISY CLASSROOM
BY IEVA FLAMINGO

Illustrated by Vivianna Maria Staņislavska
Translated by Žanete Vēvere Pasqualini,
Sara Smith and Richard O'Brien

It isn't easy being a kid – especially not in the noisiest class in the school. Some days, you struggle with algebra, or too much homework. Sometimes, one of your fellow pupils just won't SHUT UP.

When the class feels like a many-headed dragon, how can you find a place for yourself? Would you feel less lonely if you could smuggle a cat in?

RRP £8.50 / ISBN 978-1-910139-82-0
A collection of poems aimed at children aged 8+

ALSO FROM THE EMMA PRESS

MOON JUICE
BY KATE WAKELING

Illustrated by Elīna Braslipa

Meet Skig, who's meant to be a warrior (but is really more of a worrier). Meet a giddy comet, skidding across the sky with her tail on fire. Put a marvellous new machine in your pocket and maybe you'll be able to fix all your life's problems.

Kate Wakeling's first book of poems for children is full of curious characters and strange situations. The poems she writes are always musical, sometimes magical, and full of wonder at the weirdness of the world.

RRP £8.50 / ISBN 978-1-910139-49-3
A collection of poems aimed at children aged 8+